MISSING LINK

BY SANDRA MARIN

1

"Levin! Stop daydreaming and pay attention!" Cameron shouts.

I'm thinking about going home and sleeping. I haven't slept in days. I reply, "I'm awake master, what do you want?"

Cameron is annoyed, "Pay attention. I'm not repeating myself! You and Davis are going to the scene to investigate. Smith and Hunter are staying here and researching suspects."

Cameron leaves the room. Mitch coughs to get my attention. I gasp, "What?"

Mitch sighs, "You really weren't paying attention, were you?"

"I heard him call everyone by their last name!"

"Alex, you need to focus. This is serious. Ten people were shoot last night in a warehouse. Whoever did it cleaned up the mess. We have zero leads and found only a strand of a dead woman's hair left behind," Mitch puts his hand on his forehead.

I yawn, "I am focused." I am seriously tired and ready to go home.

Mitch is sarcastic, "Sure you are. I'm going to the warehouse. You can come with me, stay here, or go home and sleep!"

"Let's go," I roll my eyes.

I follow Mitch outside of the station to an SIS car. Mitch gets in the driver's side. I hop in the passengers. Mitch drives through the city.

Mitch asks, "How do you like it here anyway?"

"It's not as exciting as New York City," I reply. There was case after case and long hours. I moved to Miami because it's warmer. I thought maybe it wouldn't be as dramatic. I'm wrong.

Mitch laughs, "I bet. Of course, I wouldn't know I've been at this SIS station a while."

I gaze out the window. It is getting dark. We're out of the city of Miami. I ask, "Where is this place anyway?"

"A bit out of the city in the country," Mitch stomps on the brakes and turns into a dirt path. It leads us to the warehouse. Mitch and I get out of the car.

The warehouse is old and falling apart. It has broken windows and the entrance is shattered in pieces on the ground.

Mitch says, "That was easy." He bends down and studies the broken glass.

He continues, "Some of these pieces are covered in dirt, others are crystal clean. Odd."

Mitch leads the way in the warehouse and I follow. The warehouse is completely empty.

I sigh, "Whoever did this, knew what they were doing."

Mitch puts his hand on his chin, "Perhaps. I wonder if they have any connection to the serial killer on the run. Leanna and Nick are running background checks on criminals in the area."

I separate from Mitch and look around the warehouse. I walk into an empty room and see a old wooden chair in the corner.

Mitch yells, "Anything!?"

"No, only an old chair!" I holler back.

Mitch rushes in the room. He takes one look at the chair. He laughs, "That tells us people used to sit on their asses in here!"

I sigh, "This is a dead end. I'll make a mental note of it anyway."

Mitch asks, "Are you done here?"

I nod. Mitch and I leave the warehouse and head back to the station.

2

Mitch and I go to the security deck to see Leanna and Nick. I ask, "Find anything?"

Leanna sighs, "Not really, this is going nowhere."

Nick gasps, "What she means is, we found two suspects. One of them is the dead woman. The other one left this area years ago and resides in Ireland."

Mitch attempts to push Nick aside so he can see the screen. Nick moves.

"What are you looking at!? This is a blank screen!" Mitch raises his voice.

Nick rolls his eyes, "That's because I closed it out a minute ago, genius. We're about to go on break. Look for Isabella Trail and Duncan McArthur."

Leanna and Nick get up and leave. Mitch searches for them on the computer.

Mitch says, "Isabella Trail's body was found in a lake nearby a year ago. Duncan McArthur is from and lived in Miami his entire life until he

moved to Dublin, Ireland three years ago. It makes

no sense how they'd be connected."

I quietly analyze the screen for a moment. I

say, "Unless, Isabella isn't actually dead. Who's to

say Duncan didn't come back to the city to visit?"

"You have a point," Mitch taps his hand on

the desk.

I have an idea. I smirk. Mitch stops tapping

the desk. He says, "I know that face. Let me guess,

we're going to see what can find about them?"

"Yes, what other choice do we have?"

Nick and Leanna return from their break.

Nick stares angrily at Mitch. Nick yells, "Off my

computer! Leanna and I will look more into the two suspects and report information to you!"

Leanna tries not to laugh, "Men!"

Nick replies, "Why don't you and Mitch take a lunch? Leanna and I will get to work,"

Mitch and I go on lunch. We're the only two people in the break room. I sit next to Mitch.

Mitch asks, "What are you thinking?"

"Isabella Trail and Duncan McArthur are somewhat connected. We know nothing about them. We can't say if they would or wouldn't shoot ten people," I reply.

Mitch shrugs his shoulders, "People are sick. Maybe they had an alternative motive."

"Maybe," I have a weird feeling in my gut.

"What are you doing tonight?"

"Sleeping."

"That's not what I meant!"

"What did you mean?" I smirk.

"Some co-workers are going out for a drink."

"Eh."

"What you don't want to see Cameron drunk again?"

"I'd rather get drunk and talk to a plant myself!" We laugh.

After lunch we meet Nick and Leanna. Nick says, "We found that Isabella Trail has a daughter named Rosa Trail. Rosa lives outside of the city with her foster parents. She is fifteen years old."

"That's young," I reply.

Nick continues, "Yeah, well Isabella was thirty-one when she died. That means she had Rosa when she was sixteen. Isabella was found dead in a river not that far from her house. Hypothermia is listed as the cause of her death. Reports say she committed suicide. Isabella has a clean background. I don't see how she'd be connected to the crime if she's been dead a year."

I'm suspicious, "Why would Isabella kill herself by drowning and freezing to death in a river? We're missing something."

Mitch is quiet.

I continue, "She's also been dead a year. How could a dead person be connected to a crime unless they're not actually dead? Someone also could have connected her to it to buy themselves time. They knew we would look into it."

Mitch glances at me. He clears his voice, "You're right. I can't help but feel Isabella is being used as a distraction in this case."

Leanna coughs, "Anyway, there's more. Duncan McArthur went to high school with Isabella. Not only are they the same age, they probably also knew each other. Duncan was in Miami a month ago for a comic convention, two weeks before the homicide."

Mitch asks, "What is he doing in Ireland?"

"I don't know. That's something you should ask him. Even if he's not the guy, maybe he could help lead to him or her."

Mitch and I thank them and call it a day. We head out to our cars.

Mitch asks, "Are you coming tonight?"

I sigh, "Fine."

The work day is over. I head to my apartment. I watch crime television shows until it's time to leave.

I meet Mitch inside the bar. A bartender comes over and asks, "Can I get you something to drink?"

"Sex on the beach," I reply.

Mitch answers, "Draft beer."

We show the bartender our licenses. He winks at me, "You look young for your age."

"Thanks," I try not to laugh.

Mitch laughs, "How old are you anyway? Eighteen!?"

I hit Mitch's arm, "I'm thirty, same age as you!"

"How do you know how old I am?"

"It was written in the bathroom stalls."

"Oh, really?"

"No, it was on your SIS profile! Einstein!"

Mitch and I laugh hysterically. The bartender hands us our drinks. I look around the room and see Nick and Leanna laughing. Our other co-workers look like they're trying to avoid Cameron. Cameron spots Mitch and I.

I whisper, "Let's go."

"What!?" Mitch raises his voice.

"It's Cameron, duh. You want him to see us?"

Mitch lowers his voice, "Ah, no." Mitch grabs my hand. We walk away from the bar.

Cameron comes up behind me and grabs my shoulder. Mitch and I stop walking. Mitch is furious.

"What are you doing!?" He yells.

Cameron laughs, "I see you two are trying to get away and have a party of your own! It's Friday fun night! Come dance with the rest of us!"

I look around confused. No one is dancing. Everyone is off in little groups talking and drinking. Cameron must be drunk already. Great.

I reply, "No one is dancing. Now if you excuse us –"

Cameron cuts me off, "BORING! BORING!" He tries to grab my ass. I take a step back.

Mitch notices and pushes Cameron. Cameron attempts to punch Mitch. Mitch ducks and he misses. Cameron punches a big man that appears to be a body builder. He is furious.

Cameron attempts to run away from him. The man picks him up and throws him into a table. He yells, "Next time your punk ass touches me, you won't have any hands or legs left!"

Cameron lays scared on the ground. The bar fills with laughter. Mitch grabs my hand and pulls me outside.

I ask, "What are you doing?"

Mitch answers, "Getting you away from there."

"Why?" I laugh.

Mitch is serious, "You know, when he's done whining on the floor, he'll come back to you." Mitch lets go of my hand.

He saved me again from Cameron. This is exactly why I don't go to outings with co-workers, Cameron.

Mitch and I head to our cars. Mitch asks, "You good to drive home?"

I reply, "I only had like two sips before Cameron came over."

"Okay."

Mitch is quiet standing in front of me. He looks at me. This is awkward. I shouldn't. What the hell. We kiss.

3

I wake up to a text from Mitch telling me to meet him at the warehouse. Saturday and Sunday flew by. I get out of bed and head to the warehouse.

I see Mitch's car parked outside. I get out of my car and walk into the building.

Mitch is looking at something on the wall. I ask, "Anything."

Mitch replies, "No, not yet anyway. This is an old building with dirty walls."

I study the wall for a minute. Yeah, so there's some dirt on it. What's his point? I ask, "Okay, so it's a dirty wall? What are you trying to accomplish by looking at it?"

Mitch is quiet for a moment. He receives a text. Mitch reads it and says, "This."

He shows me a message from Leanna. It says that Isabella Trail has a living daughter named Rosa.

Mitch clears his voice, "Well, I was waiting for them to come back with more information and at the same time, avoid Cameron."

Here I'd thought everyone would forget what happened Friday. I was wrong.

Mitch continues, "Anyway, she doesn't live that far from here. We should go speak to her."

I nod, "Yeah."

Mitch and I walk out of the warehouse. Mitch suggests, "Come with me, leave your car here. We'll be back."

Mitch and I get in his car. He types an address in his phone and drives off. I look around. We're in the country. It's so beautiful, quiet, and peaceful out here. The houses we drive by are yards apart.

Mitch pulls in a driveway. The house is enormous. I'm nervous, "What now? They can look out the window and see us."

"Yeah, so, we're here to be seen," Mitch smirks.

I still have an unsettling feeling about this. Mitch gets out the car. I follow him to the front door. He rings the doorbell.

An old woman answers the door, "You're not CPS, I hope?"

That's oddly suspicious. She must not have a clue we're investigators. Mitch clears his voice, "No, ma'am. We're not. Are you expecting them anytime soon?"

The woman looks nervous, "No, of course not. Who are you then?"

I answer, "We're part of SIS, secret investigative services. We have a few questions for Rosa Trail, if you don't mind."

"Excuse me? She is a minor!" the lady gasps.

"It's about her mother," Mitch says.

The woman is about to shut the door in our face. A teenager cuts in front of her. The woman yells, "Rosa! No!"

Rosa slams the door behind her. It's awkward. Mitch questions, "Ah, I guess you heard us? I'm Mitchell Davis and she's Alexandria Levine. We're federal agents but we come in peace."

I laugh, "Mitch and Alex. You want to go somewhere else to talk?"

Rosa looks at Mitch and I weird. She says, "Like where? There's nothing within miles of here."

Mitch suggests, "Let's go for a ride and talk then."

"Fine, anything to get away from here," Rosa rolls her eyes.

We all get in the car. Mitch drives.

Mitch asks, "So, you know who we are and why we're here?"

Rosa sighs, "Yeah, yeah my mother. I never met her. She committed suicide a year ago. That's all I know. I know you did a background check on her, that's how you found me and you know she was sixteen when she had me. That's why she gave me away. There's nothing else to it, why can't you leave me alone?"

I reply, "You're right, we ran a background check. Not because of her death, she was reported as dead and is a suspect for a crime. We think it's possible she was framed, or could be perhaps; alive but reported as dead."

"What!? No way! That only happens in television shows!" Rosa is amused.

Mitch coughs, "Anyway, anything you know may be helpful. If you know anything, of course."

Rosa says, "I don't. I lived with Becky and John since I was born. I asked if I could meet her someday and they said it'd probably be a bad idea. They think it'd hurt me."

"Why?" I ask.

Rosa shrugs her shoulders, "I don't know. They thought she'd have some family or be something I wouldn't expect. It'd be for my own good if I didn't know. I mean, we never met after all."

I feel sorry for Rosa. I don't want to keep asking her questions about her mother. Clearly, she doesn't know anything. That's all we can use towards the investigation.

"I want to believe she only got rid of me because she couldn't support me being sixteen. I don't think if I got pregnant in a year, I could either. That I understand. It sucks but it's life," Rosa shrugs her shoulders.

Mitch appears to be deep in thought. He asks, "How are Becky and John to you?" Finally, he's shifting gears and not talking about her mother.

"They're okay. Becky is forgetful and overprotective. John hardly gets up from the couch," Rosa answers.

"You live with other kids?"

"Wendy, Casey, Tyler, and Harold. I'm the oldest."

I have a strange feeling. I wonder why

Becky thought we were child protective services. I

hesitate, "Have you heard of CPS?"

"Yeah, they were over at the house last

week because Tyler and Harold showed up to

school with bruises on their fast after getting in a

fight on the bus."

"Becky and John have never touched you?"

"No. They're old and boring. I'm not even

allowed to hangout with my boys that are my

friends after school," Rosa sighs.

That's a relief. Then we'd have to report

them for child abuse and we don't want to deal with

that on top of this case. Mitch pulls in Rosa's

driveway. We thank her for talking to us and wish

her luck in finishing the school year. We head back to the warehouse.

I get out of Mitch's car and say, "I'll see you back at the station. We need to figure out what's next."

Mitch waves and leaves. I get in my car and head to the station. I walk in the entrance and see Cameron. He comes up to me.

He says, "I'm not sure what happened Friday night, but I'm sorry. Can we keep what happened between us a secret? If my boss finds out about it, he'll be furious."

I'm amused yet pretend, "I don't know what you're talking about."

"Okay, then. Take care," Cameron winks at me and walks off. I roll my eyes.

I meet Mitch in his office. I ask, "What now?"

Mitch sighs, "I guess the only other thing for us to do right now, is go to Ireland."

"Ireland!? For what?" I exclaim.

"The only other person we can speak to right now is Duncan. I thought you'd be more thrilled to leave here. You want to stay here with Cameron?".

"I'm good."

"Tomorrow we will fly out. I'll report to Cameron."

I can't help but feel like there's something Mitch is hiding. I don't know what. Maybe it'll come out in Ireland.

4

I meet Mitch at the airport in the morning. Mitch and I get in line to aboard the plane. I sit next to him on the plane. Mitch says, "You look nervous."

I roll my eyes, "I'm not nervous, I'm anxious. I feel like this is a dead end."

"Maybe, maybe not."

Mitch and I are quiet the rest of the flight. The plane lands. We're in Ireland. It's dark out. Mitch and I take a taxi to a hotel.

We walk up to the front desk. Mitch says, "Room for Davis."

The employee hands Mitch a key. I start to speak, "Ro—"

Mitch cuts me off, "You're with me."

"Why?" I ask under my breath.

Mitch grabs my arm, "C'mon. I had too, they didn't have any other rooms available."

We go in the room. There's only one bed. Great.

I'm sarcastic, "I hope you're planning to sleep on the floor."

"That's the best I could do, besides I know you want me," Mitch winks.

I roll my eyes, "Whatever. Can we just go to bed?"

Mitch and I get ready for bed and fall asleep. In the morning I wake with his arm wrapped around me. I take his arm off my shoulder.

It startles him, "What?"

I laugh, "Sorry, princess. I didn't know you were still sleeping!"

Mitch is embarrassed.

I question, "You know where we're going?"

"Yeah, yeah, I made note of it on my phone," Mitch jumps out of bed.

We both get ready and leave. Mitch and I take a taxi to Duncan's house. Duncan's house is huge.

Mitch rings the doorbell. A tall muscular man with red hair answers it. It must be Duncan.

He says, "I'm not expecting company. Who are you?"

Mitch asks, "Are you Duncan McArthur?"

The man is cocky, "Yes, who might you be? Private investigators?"

"Yes, exactly. That's who we are!" Mitch raises his voice.

Duncan slams the door in our face.

I whisper, "Nice going, Mitch. What are going to do now?"

"Wait. One, two, th—"

"Why are you here?" Duncan opens to door.

I answer, "You're a suspect for a crime in America. We're wondering if you have any connection to Isabella Trail."

"What!?" Duncan is shocked and waves us in. His house is neat and enormous.

He apologizes, "I'm sorry, my place is a mess. My maid is on vacation."

Mitch is impressed, "You have a maid?"

"Yes, course," Duncan laughs.

We take a seat in his living room.

Duncan is serious, "I know you're all investigators and all but can I ask you something? Why the hell am I suspect for a crime!?"

Mitch sighs, "The only leads we have right now are you and Isabella Trail. Isabella died a year ago. You were in Miami two weeks before the homicide."

Duncan is surprised, "Isabella is dead!?"

"You didn't know?"

"Of course not. I don't even know what homicide you're talking about. Yes, I was in Miami a while ago. I was visiting some old friends and discussing business."

I ask, "What business?"

Duncan smirks, "You mean to tell me you did a background check and didn't find out I own a major car manufacturing company!? La Moore, ring a bell? I'm thinking of starting one in the United States and my old friend, Aaron Walters is looking for a partner."

"Interesting. Did you happen to stop at a warehouse?"

"I don't know what warehouse you're talking about. I went to a comic convention. Otherwise, I spent most of my time in Miami on beaches. You know, it is rainy weather here in Dublin lately."

Mitch sighs, "Sorry, whoever ran background checks pulled up your name. Will you excuse me a moment?"

Duncan nods. Mitch takes his phone out of his pocket and steps out of the room.

Duncan asks, "What is it?"

I reply, "He's probably asking Leanna or Nick why they pulled up your name. The report only shows a strand of Isabella's hair."

"Isabella is alive?"

"We honestly can't answer that."

Mitch enters the room. He sits down next to me, "One of our other investigators back home says your name was pulled up because of your connection with Isabella. When he searched Isabella Trail's name, you were the first to come up in an article. So, if there's a person that knows anything about her, it'd be you."

Duncan is quiet for a moment. He finally says, "Oh, yeah. We dated in high school. We were in the French club. They took pictures for the yearbook. Maybe they published an article about it, I don't know. All of this is news to me."

"You didn't kill her?" Mitch asks.

Duncan is annoyed, "As I said, all of this is news to me. I didn't know she was dead. I know nothing about whatever happened in the warehouse in Miami. Why don't you track down some of my old friends? They used to hang out there, I didn't."

Mitch sighs, "Fine." He opens a notes application on his phone.

Duncan clears his voice, "Randy Philips, Oliver Turner, Blake Silverstone, Kelly White, Emma Richardson, and Josh Richardson."

Mitch looks at the list he created. He says, "That's a lot of names."

"Yeah, most of them I played football with in high school. There was only a few I enjoyed seeing outside of school and football," Duncan shrugs his shoulders.

I apologize, "I'm sorry, this is all news to you. If there's any other information you have that'd be helpful, don't hesitate to tell us."

Duncan replies, "Not really. Isabella and I dated. My friends thought she was weird and an outcast but I didn't care. We fell in love and broke up days before the prom. She said she was moving. I didn't believe her. I haven't seen her since."

I wonder if Duncan is Rosa's father and if the reason Isabella left was because she was pregnant? If only Isabella was alive, I would know more.

"I'm sorry to hear that," I apologize.

Mitch and I look at each other. We both stand up. Mitch says, "I guess that is all we have for you for now."

"You're not going to arrest me?" Duncan asks.

Mitch and I laugh. I answer, "No, we don't have evidence to arrest you. We'll go through the list of names you gave us and go from there."

Mitch and I thank Duncan and leave. Mitch calls a taxi. While we wait, he calls Nick.

Nick answers sarcastically, "What do you want!?"

Mitch laughs, "I have a list of names I want you and Leanna to look into."

"Can you text or email them to me? I have my hands tied at the moment."

"Yes, talk to you later."

"Bye."

The call ends. Mitch sends Nick a text. The taxi arrives. The driver asks where we're going.

Mitch replies, "Hotel West."

I ask, "Why are we going back there?"

"We have to get our stuff and check out before we go to the airport. Besides, I only booked the room for one night."

The taxi stops at the hotel. Mitch and I gather our things. Mitch checks out of the hotel. We walk down the street to a bus station. We take the bus to the airport. Our flight number is called the moment we arrive. Mitch and I aboard a plane back to Miami.

When we walk out of the airport, Mitch receives a text from Nick. He reads it.

Mitch says, "Randy Philips, Oliver Turner, Kelly White, and Emma Richardson have a clean background. Blake Silverstone robbed two liquor stores in the past. Emma Richardson is Josh Richardson's ex-wife. Josh was arrested for attempting to murder a cop and robbing a liquor store."

I'm impressed, "That was fast."

Mitch puts his hand on his chin. It's quiet when we walk to his car. We get in the car. Mitch says, "I can't help but feel Blake and Josh are connected."

I sigh, "It still doesn't explain anything."

"I'll message Duncan and ask him."

"You have his number?"

"I got it on the way out, you obviously weren't paying attention."

5

Mitch drops me off home. I spend the rest of my day watching television. I pass out on the couch.

I wake up to a text that says, "Meet me at the warehouse."

I realize I forgot my car phone driver at the station. I stop by work to pick it up. I don't see any sign of Cameron. I'm relieved. I leave and meet Mitch at the warehouse.

Mitch says, "Duncan messaged me back last night. He said Blake and Josh were best friends. Blake followed Josh though he didn't agree with him. Duncan remembers the time they robbed a liquor store. Josh asked him to do it with him and he refused. Blake went with him. Since then they stopped hanging out but they were part of the same group and had to be civil."

"Wow, okay. I'm glad you made me drive out here to tell me this," I'm sarcastic.

Mitch is agitated, "If you could have managed to be on time this morning, you would have known that Cameron had cops in his office. I told you to come out here to get away from there. Maybe we'll find something we missed here."

I'm confused, "Why would Cameron have cops in his office?"

"Someone reported him for sexual assault, can we get back to the case?"

"Fine," I cross my arms and roll my eyes. Mitch ignores me and walks away.

I head back to the room with the chair. I kick it over. I see an old piece of gum under it. Great. Our next clue is a piece of gum. I'm not touching it with my bare hands. I see a small piece of paper in the corner of the room. I pick it up and use it to get the gum off the chair. I roll the gum in the paper and put it in my pocket.

I look around for Mitch and can't find him. I walk around the warehouse and see a small hallway. The hallway has a bathroom at the end. I peak in the bathroom and see Mitch. I startle him.

Mitch jumps, "What are you doing here!?"

I'm sarcastic, "I wanted to see you take a piss."

Mitch tries not to laugh.

I continue, "You're jumpy."

Mitch smirks, "I'm not, you are!"

"Did you find anything or no?"

"There's some mold on the walls."

"Gross."

Mitch reaches in his pocket and takes out a ring, "I also found this."

I look at it. It's shaped like a heart and covered in dirt. I say, "That's something. All I found is an old piece of gum."

"Did you save it?" Mitch puts the ring back in his pocket.

"Unfortunately. We'll bring it to the lab and see if they can find any DNA on it."

"I also had Nick track down Blake and Josh. Blake is a doctor and Josh owns a clothing line called Cloud Five."

"A doctor?"

"Yes."

"Why would a doctor kill someone?"

"I'm thinking the same thing. I mean it happens, look at Hollywood."

"We're not in Hollywood," I check the time on my phone.

I say, "We're a few hours in our shift."

Mitch thinks for a moment, "Let's go to the hospital. We have no idea how long it'll take. You can follow my car."

"Whatever."

Mitch and I leave. I follow him to a hospital. We walk in to the front desk. Mitch asks, "May I speak to doctor Silverstone?"

The receptionist says, "Do you have an appointment?"

"No."

"I can't let you in without an appointment."

Mitch whispers to me, "Distract her, I have an idea."

I ask the receptionist, "Do you have any planned parenthood classes here?"

She replies, "I don't think so, this isn't the OGYN."

"I heard hospitals sometimes have classes like that. My fiancé and I are planning to have a baby."

"I can check that for you, hold on a second," the receptionist types some things on her computer.

Mitch sneaks in behind her. He quickly looks through a folder. He winks at me. I see the receptionist isn't paying attention to me. I duck and head towards the door. I meet Mitch on the other side.

I whisper, "Where are we going?"

Mitch hushes me, "Quiet. We still don't have visitor passes and they have cameras everywhere. I was able to find the room number he's at."

I follow Mitch. He stops at a room labeled, "Seventy." Mitch peaks inside.

He whispers, "Only Blake is in there. It looks like he's finishing up some notes."

Mitch knocks on the door. No answer. We quietly enter the room. Blake looks up from his notes at us. He says, "Can I help you?"

Mitch hesitates, "We have a few questions for you when you have time."

"Who are you? Do I need to call security?"

Blake stands up.

Mitch stands frozen with his mouth shut. Great. It looks like I'm handling this one. I answer, "We're with the SIS. We know you have a connection with Josh Richardson."

"Great, what did he do now?"

"It's not to say he did anything. We're investigating a crime north of here."

"Okay, make it quick. I don't have much time today. We need to get out of this room."

Blake steps out of the room. Mitch and I follow. Blake leads us to an empty lobby.

Blake lowers his voice, "Josh and I used to be friends back in the day. We fell out years ago when he tricked me into robbing a liquor store with him. We still have mutual friends, however. I don't even know what crime you're talking about. If I could help you more, I would. I have surgery in a few minutes." Blake scratches his forehead. I believe he's telling the truth.

Blakes eyes light up, "I know what you're talking about! A patient of mine mentioned it the other day. Someone fired a gun at the warehouse off Bay road."

I reply, "Yeah, that's it!"

"We used to hangout there as teenagers. I haven't been there a long time. Anyway, I need to get going. If you need anything else, you know where to find me!" Blake leaves the lobby.

Mitch stares at me, "Are you thinking what I'm thinking?"

My mind is blank. Wait, the last two people have led us to Josh. I reply, "Maybe."

Mitch blurts, "Josh!"

"Yes," I nod.

Mitch and I head back to the station. We go over some notes during lunch such as what were going to ask Josh and where his business is. Mitch searches for it and writes it down. After lunch we get into a SIS car. Mitch drives as I type the address in GPS.

6

We go through the city of Miami and stop at a big building. Mitch and I get out of the car and step into the building.

The receptionist greets us, "Hello, how may I help you? Do you have an appointment?"

Mitch and I stare at each other confused.

"Any time today," she smirks.

I finally answer, "We're looking for Josh Richardson."

"You've come to the right place. He doesn't see anyone without an appointment. Are you the new intern?"

"Yes," I lie.

"What about your boyfriend? It doesn't look like he wants to you to go to work without him!"

Mitch tries not to laugh, "New job, new city. I wouldn't want my girlfriend walking her by herself so I gave her a ride."

"And you had to escort her in too? So cute," the receptionist smiles.

She continues, "Floor two, room three. He just got out of a meeting. I'm sure he's looking forward to meeting you!"

I walk ahead of Mitch. He winks at the receptionist. I can't believe she bought that. Everyone but me wants to believe chivalry isn't dead. Mitch and I step into an elevator. It is slow.

Mitch jokes, "My girlfriend, what do you want to do later?"

"Nothing with you," I laugh.

"You're one of the girls that go home to their nine cats?"

"I don't have cats. At least I don't go home to my nine girlfriends!"

The elevator stops. Saved by the bell. Mitch and I get out of the elevator and find room three.

Mitch knocks on the door. A short muscular man opens it. He is suspicious, "Who are you? You're not my lunch!"

Mitch laughs, "Of course not. You must be Josh Richardson?"

He is sarcastic, "It depends, who is asking?"

I cross my arms and raise my voice, "We're federal agents Mr. Richardson. You're a suspect for a crime!"

Josh sits down at his desk. Mitch and I enter the room. I lock the door behind me.

Josh is furious, "Unless you have a warrant, I'm not speaking to you. I'm going to call security."

Mitch hits his fist on the desk, "This is serious. If you don't start talking, we will find a way to put you behind bars fast."

"I don't see how, but okay humor me," Josh chuckles.

"What is your relationship with Duncan McArthur?" Mitch asks.

Josh rolls his eyes, "Duncan was one of my friends back in the day before he was sleeping with my ex, Isabella Trail."

I question, "You and Isabella were dating?"

"We dated a really long time ago. I don't know what you people want from me. I didn't kill anyone."

Mitch is curious, "Why do you still hang around Duncan after all these years?"

"I like to play poker with Randy, Oliver, and Kelly. Sometimes, Duncan is there."

"What about Blake? Or Isabella?"

"What about him? We used to be best friends. Isabella and I dated before Duncan transferred to the school. She wanted to take a break because we were moving too fast. I walked by Duncan's house and saw them in his wind–"

I cut him off, "What about Isabella?"

Duncan raises his voice, "If you let me continue, I tried to avoid Duncan as much as possible after that. I didn't see Isabella around either. Rumors hit that she was pregnant, killed herself, joined a cult, or ran away."

"Why would she run away?" I wonder. I don't know much about Isabella yet.

Josh shrugs his shoulders, "I don't know. You know teenagers assume shit based on appearance. She always wore black and didn't talk much in school. I knew she argued a lot with her parents and stayed away from home as much as possible. She stayed with friends or camped out in the library after school."

Mitch receives a text on his phone. He's angry, "You better start talking."

I lean over to Mitch and whisper, "What?"

He shows me the text from Nick. The old piece of gum in the warehouse has Josh's DNA on it.

Josh stares at us confused.

Mitch raises his voice, "Explain why your piece of gum was found at the warehouse!?"

"What are you talking about!?" Josh exclaims.

Mitch yells, "What were you doing in the warehouse?"

"I haven't been to any warehouse since I was a teenager! I'm not talking to you anymore without a lawyer!"

"Mitch checks the time on his phone. He says, "You're lucky it's getting late. You'll be hearing from us again.""

Mitch and I leave the building and travel back to the station. We get out of the car and wave goodbye. I head home and go straight to bed.

I struggle to fall asleep. I feel like we're missing something. Isabella Trail. Who are you? I eventually fall asleep. I dream.

There's a woman with black hair passed out on a ground. A man wearing a mask and dressed in black carries her to a body of water. He throws her body in the water and walks off. The woman gets out of the water and yells, "Help!" There's not a single person nearby.

The alarm on my phone wakes me. Was that Isabella? Could it be she wasn't dead!?

7

I meet Mitch, Nick, and Leanna in a laboratory. They're looking at the old piece of gum and heart shaped ring. Mitch says, "I have a feeling the ring may be connected somehow. I wonder if Duncan knows anything about it."

I reply, "Text him, genius."

I analyze the gum. I look at Nick, "The gum looks pretty old and gross. Can you date it?"

Nick sighs, "That I can't do. Maybe one of the scientists can."

"We spoke to Josh yesterday; he was in the warehouse back in the day."

Leanna gasps, "What about the ring!?"

Nick replies, "We have no information about it yet."

Mitch receives a text. He reads it. Mitch says, "Duncan says the ring looks familiar. He thinks it was Isabella's and he never bought her a ring."

I question, "Why would we find Isabella's ring in the warehouse? Unless, of course she was there at a point."

Nick sighs, "Maybe if we could date them, we could point to a time. We already have Josh. We don't know for sure if it's Isabella's ring. I'll contact Steve when he's out of meeting."

Leanna is confused, "Who is Steve!?"

"The only person who can date these," Nick strolls through his notes on the computer. Leanna watches him and sighs.

Mitch winks at me. He heads out of the laboratory. I'm confused yet follow him anyway.

"What?" I ask under my breath.

Mitch says, "Nothing. We need to get out of here."

"Where would we go? Back to the warehouse?"

Mitch smiles, "I have an idea."

We get in Mitch's car. He drives through the city, pass the warehouse, and into the country. He stops at a metal gate. It looks like an entrance to the woods.

Mitch pulls his car up next to the gate. We get out of the car. Mitch walks ahead of me and I follow. We walk around some trees and avoid the gate.

I'm confused, "What are we doing here?"

Mitch says, "The river Isabella died in is in these woods."

"I'm not sure if I ever heard of river running through the woods in the middle of nowhere!"

Mitch laughs, "You're obviously a city folk! You know, this place used to be a town!"

"What makes you think I'm from the city?" I'm annoyed.

"It's obvious you aren't from here. If you were, you would have known that!"

"You are?"

"Yes."

I look around the woods. This place is dark and creepy. I wouldn't be surprised if it's haunted.

Mitch starts to tell a story. Sometime hundreds of years ago the woods were a town called Redwood. Beaver lake was a place where residents would fish, swim, and have boating races. The lake used to extend to the major bodies of water but over time shrunk. People went off to war or moved when their crops started dying. It turned into an abandoned drought. Then eventually, was flooded.

I look up to the sky. It is turning rain.

Mitch sighs, "Anyway, this used to be a good place a long time ago. Now it's nothing but trees and wildlife."

I reply, "So, I have to worry about animals possibly attacking me and getting soaked?"

Mitch laughs, "You'll be fine, the trees are big enough to be an umbrella!"

"At least it's warm out, I won't freeze. I'm not from the city originally, by the way."

"Really? You were in New York City last."

"Yeah, I worked at a SIS station there for a year. Then I saw there was an opening in Miami and applied."

"Why?"

"It's warmer, for one. It was too chaotic there. I'm from Sky, Oklahoma."

"Never heard of it."

"That's because it has a population of a thousand at most."

"So, you're used to getting soaked?" We laugh.

Mitch and I continue to walk through the woods until we come across a body of water. It looks too small and shallow to be a river.

I ask, "You sure this is the river?"

Mitch shrugs his shoulders, "That's what the report says. I guess it dried up again."

"I thought you were from this area, wouldn't you know?"

"No, I left a long time ago after my father passed."

"I'm sorry."

Mitch studies the lake, "It looks like a swamp."

"Want to step in and see if you find any leeches?" I laugh.

"Sure!" Mitch is sarcastic.

We hear footsteps behind us. A voice startles us, "What are you two doing here!?" Mitch and I turn around and see a man in hunting gear.

I'm anxious, "We're doing an investigation."

The man laughs, "Really? Are you the police? You need to tell me if you are!"

Mitch smirks, "No man, not the kind you're thinking of. We investigate crimes."

"Interesting, nobody comes to Beaver lake for anything expect to hunt."

Mitch and I look at each as if we're studying who is going to respond. I finally do, "Have you heard of Isabella Trial?"

"Yeah, yeah. Every person that comes here has. Some say they see her wandering the woods."

Chills go up my spine, "You mean actually her or her spirit?"

"Who knows. I've seen a lady once; maybe it was her. Creepy as hell. What are you investigating anyway? How she died? That was a while ago."

The man seems to know his stuff. Mitch answers him, "More like, why she's connected to a crime if she's supposedly dead."

The man laughs, "Oh, yeah I've seen this shit on tv! The evil spirit emerges and kills people to get revenge!"

Mitch rolls his eyes, "Only in television shows, this is real life!"

The man coughs and takes a rifle off his back. He says, "Alright then. I'm going to hunt. You two stand clear. This is not a place you want to be unarmed!"

The man walks by us. Mitch and I stare at each other. It begins to rain. Mitch says, "C'mon let's go."

Mitch leads the way. I trip on a rock and fall. Mitch continues to walk and doesn't notice me.

I feel something push me up. I turn around. I see a woman with long black hair behind me.

I'm terrified, "Who are you? Isa—"

The woman laughs, "Bella."

"What do you want? Are you alive or dead?"

"I am married to these woods."

"What does that mean?" I look at her face. Her face is pale and dirty. Her eyes are black. She disappears in front of me. It's apparent, that was her spirit.

I look around and don't see Mitch anywhere. I hear a gun shot. I run through the woods. I have no idea where I'm going but I hope it leads me out.

I see Mitch by the entrance waiting for me. I run up to him. I yell, "What the hell!? I tripped on a rock and you left me in the woods!"

Mitch replies, "Last I knew you were behind me. Then I made it to the entrance, turned around and saw you running."

I try to catch my breath, "I saw Isabella. I saw her spirit. She is dead. She said she is married to the woods."

Mitch questions, "Really?"

"Yes, you have to believe me."

"Whether I believe you or not, we can't use a spirit in our investigation. We need to figure out why her DNA was found at the crime. Especially, if she died a year ago. Something doesn't add up."

Another gun shot comes from the woods. The rain and wind picks up.

I sigh, "Yeah, yeah. We need to get out of here."

Mitch nods. We head to his car and leave. Mitch receives a phone call from Duncan. He presses the a button labeled Redwire and answers it, "Hello?"

Duncan replies, "I bet you weren't expecting to hear me. I'm driving, I have Redwire I figured I'd give you a quick call. I hope I'm not interrupting anything."

"Not at all, we're heading back to the station."

"Anyway, I remembered something important that might help. You know that ring you sent me a picture of?"

"Yeah."

"I remember that Isabella said it was from Josh and she didn't take it off because he threatened to kill her. The last time I saw her she was wearing that. I wondered if she was cheating on me with him but no, the next day Josh was at school making out with some girl."

"We are investigating Josh right now. That is some useful information my friend, thank you."

I wonder if should mention Isabella had a daughter. It could be his. It's not my business but if I never see him again, he'd probably never know.

Duncan replies, "Any –"

I cut him off, "I think there's something you should if we never speak to you again. There is a girl named Rosa Trail, Isabella had her when she was sixteen. We believe the reason she didn't show up to school anymore was because she was pregnant."

Duncan is shocked, "I see, am the father? What about Josh!?"

"We don't know. I'm just telling you the reason she didn't show up anymore."

"Should I get a DNA test?"

"It's up to you."

"What would you do Mitch?"

Mitch replies, "I'm not sure if we should be meddling into family affairs but I like you and you helped us."

Duncan laughs.

"Why not? It won't hurt." Mitch answers.

We arrive at the station. Mitch says, "Okay, we're at the station. Good luck with everything. I hope if we do talk again, it's not about this case. Thank you."

"Thank you," I say.

The call ends. Mitch and I go inside the station. I ask, "What now?"

He replies, "We look more at Josh until Nick and Leanna come back with more information."

8

Mitch and I are on computers next to each other. Mitch asks, "What is Josh's last name again?"

I answer, "Richardson."

Only a few things come up. Mitch says, "Yeah, yeah we know that he robbed a liquor store when he was a teenager."

I see an article about outdoor track come up. I quickly go skim through it. I say, "He also ran track in high school. So what?"

Mitch laughs, "He was fast."

An old picture of Josh pops up on the screen. I study it so he used to a lot bigger.

Mitch stands up and stretches, "I'm going to get a drink out of the vending machine, want anything?"

I shake my head. Mitch leaves the room. I continue to search for Josh Richardson. I find nothing.

Mitch comes back. He sits next to me and says, "I received a phone call from Nick when I left the room. It turns out the ring and gum date back to fifteen years ago. So, although we may be able to link Isabella and Josh, we cannot connect them to the crime. The only physical evidence we have from the scene is a strand of Isabella's hair."

I sigh, "We're missing something. From the beginning, what would motivate a person to kill random people in a dead warehouse?"

Mitch agrees, "You're right. We have no leads on who the killer is or what motivated him or her. An old ring and a piece of gum are the only clues we ha—"

"We need to go back to the warehouse!" I cut Mitch off.

"Yeah," Mitch nods.

I check the time on my phone. My shift is over in a few minutes. I wave goodbye to Mitch and head home.

I receive a text from an odd number. It reads, "You better stay away from my man or else."

I reply, "Who is this?"

"Like you don't know."

I'm confused and have a weird feeling in my stomach. Great now someone I don't know is threatening me. At least tomorrow is Saturday.

I receive a text from Mitch in the morning. I read it. He wants to meet me at the park. I hop out of bed, get ready and leave.

I meet Mitch at the park. I say, "You know it's Saturday?"

Mitch smirks, "We never stop working!"

"This better be good because we aren't getting paid for today!" I gasp.

"It is, I received a text last night from an odd number telling me to keep you away. Away from what?"

"Someone's man apparently. I received an odd text last night too."

"I figure this is a pretty public park. If someone is following us, we'd be able to catch him or her."

"If you say so."

Mitch and I walk around the park. We see children playing, flying kites, joggers, and people riding bicycles. Nothing out of the ordinary.

I sigh, "This is a bust."

"Yeah, I guess I'll see you Monday," Mitch agrees.

Mitch and I separate. Later that night, I meet up with Leanna for drinks.

Leanna asks, "So, how are things with you and Mitch?"

I laugh, "What do you mean!?"

"I saw how you two walked off that night after Cameron tried to get his nasty hands on you," Leanna grins.

I roll my eyes, "Mitch and I are partners in this investigation. Nothing more. What happened to Cameron anyway? I haven't seen him around in a while."

The waiter comes over and hands us our drinks. Leanna takes a sip, "Stop trying to change the subject. I see the way Mitch looks at you."

I shrug my shoulders and start drinking.

Leanna continues, "We aren't getting any younger! If we ever want to have kids, we need to do it before we're forty!"

I laugh hysterically, "I don't want kids!"

Leanna gulps down the rest of her drink, "Whatever. If you were around the station more, you'd know that Cameron got fired for sexual assault."

"Who did he sexually assault?" I ask.

"Besides you, one of the new ladies that work in the laboratory who happens to be the daughter of his boss."

I take another sip of my drink and spit it out. Nasty. What is it, straight Vodka? Leanna and I laugh.

I see a strange woman sitting in a bar stool across the restaurant looking at us. She has dark blue hair and a tear drop tattoo under her eye. She sticks her middle finger up at me.

I get up and walk towards her. She gets up and storms out of the door. I run after her. I hear Leanna yell behind me, "Where are you going!?"

I continue to run down the street after the lady. She stops at a bus station. I sneak behind a tree and wait for the bus to come. She gets on it. I step on the bus last.

The lady sits in the back. She sees me coming towards her and attempts to get out of her seat. I jump in the seat and block her from leaving.

I question, "Who are you? Why were you flipping me off?"

The lady is mad, "The question is who are you? Why are you around my man!?"

"What man?" I smirk.

"Josh."

I laugh hysterically.

She shouts, "Stop it! I will kill you! It's not funny!"

I stop laughing, "Yes, it is. I'm a federal agent investigating Josh. Unless you want me to investigate you too, I'd recommend keeping your mouth shut and stop sending me texts!"

The lady is quiet for a moment. She's nervous, "Are you going to put me to jail?"

"If I have reason too, you better start talking!" I raise my voice.

"Fine. My name is Veronica. I am Josh's girlfriend. I know nothing about Josh being connected to any crime. Then, again there's a lot I apparently don't know. I caught him a few days ago making out with some girl in the office. She had the same color hair as you."

Veronica is upset. I'm trying to think of something to say. I have nothing. Veronica continues, "So I thought the girl was you. I didn't notice your boyfriend at first. I wondered if he knew, it is possible. Josh has been with people in open relationships."

I try not to laugh, "Mitch and I aren't together. We're partners in this investigation."

Veronica apologizes, "I'm sorry, I didn't know. I wasn't going to go after you but a guy gave me your number."

"What guy?"

"I don't know. I was at the bar rambling about how I saw Josh with a redhead and blonde. This guy showed up next to me and started drinking. He asked me more questions about what you two looked like. I said you both wore black and look like you're on a mission of some sort."

"Okay, did the guy tell you his name?"

"I don't remember, I had too much tequila. Chris? Craig? Cameron?"

"Cameron!" I raise my voice.

"Yeah, him creepy as hell. The way he talked; I swear he had some kind of fixation with you two."

"Before you leave, may I ask you a question?"

"Sure."

"Does Josh have any enemies?"

"Not that I know of. There was this guy named Edwin he'd argue with on the phone sometimes."

The bus slows down and stops. Veronica says, "Well, that's my stop. I'm sorry again. I hope I was able to help somewhat."

I move out of the seat. Veronica gets up. I thank her and wave goodbye. She gets off the bus.

I stay on the bus until the end of the line and take a taxi home.

9

The rest of the weekend flies by. I wake up to a text message from Mitch telling me to meet him at the warehouse. I get ready for work and leave.

I pull up to the warehouse and see Mitch getting out of his car. We walk up to the entrance. Mitch studies the glass on the ground.

He says, "I know we've already established this was here for some time. Whose to say there isn't blood or something else left behind? We know the killer was clean but maybe, he or she left something behind."

"Okay, when you do that I'm going to look around," I walk pass Mitch through the entrance.

I walk around the warehouse and see nothing out of the ordinary. What is the point in coming back here? We're not finding anything.

I go back to the entrance to see Mitch. Mitch says, "Underneath the glass is more glass."

Mitch pulls a business card out from under the glass, "And this."

I read it, "Edwin Yemen. That's the guy Veronica told me about."

"Who is Veronica?" Mitch is confused.

As we head to our cars, I tell him what happened over the weekend.

Mitch says, "I think we need to separate today."

I ask, "Why?"

"It'll speed things up. I'm going to find this Edwin guy and you're going to speak to Josh."

"Why do I have to speak to Josh!?"

"If I do, I'll end up in jail. We'll report back."

"Okay."

Mitch and I separate. Before I leave, I search for Josh's business on my phone. It's going to be fun trying to sneak in without Mitch.

I walk in to the front desk. I say, "I'm here to see Josh."

The receptionist replies, "Ah yes, you must be the new assistant. He has a new office, third on the left." Last time I was the new intern now I'm the new assistant, Josh must go through employees. Not surprising.

I nod and thank the receptionist. That was easier than I thought. I open the door. Josh is on the phone. He sees me and hangs up.

He taps his fingers on the desk and laughs, "I see you can't get enough of me!"

I shut and lock the door behind me. I'm sarcastic, "Yeah, your girlfriend and I can't!"

Josh is shocked, "What do you know about Veronica!?"

"Start talking," I'm furious and wish I had a gun on me.

"Veronica wasn't at the warehouse that day."

"What day?"

Josh is nervous. He taps his foot on the floor. I receive a phone call from Mitch. I lower my voice, "Hurry up, I can't talk right now."

Mitch is quiet, "Okay. I found out Edwin was one of the guys killed in the warehouse that night and Josh's DNA was found on the card. I'll be there with backup>"

The call ends.

Josh yells, "What are you going to do arrest me!?" He picks up his phone.

I smirk, "What are you going to do now? Call a lawyer?"

"Yes, that's exactly what I'm going to do after I call security!" Josh hits a button on his phone.

I reach in my pocket and hit the record application on my phone. I say, "Go ahead, call whoever you want."

Josh laughs hysterically, "They'll be here in a minute. They're busy with your friend downstairs."

I hope Mitch didn't seriously come here by himself.

I'm about to question Josh and he brags, "Cloud Five is the best fashion line in Miami. It's only a matter of time before it's the in the country! I did pretty damn good. For you to even question me, says a lot about you so called federal agents. I work hard, I play hard I en—"

I cut him off, "I don't care what you do in your personal time Mr. Richardson. You are a suspect to a crime. Tell me what YOUR DNA was doing at the warehouse on Edwin's business card!?"

Josh laughs hysterically, "Isn't it your job to answer those questions? Man, you suck! Edwin was obviously my business partner. We were at the warehouse going over business."

"With ten other people?" I question him.

"Yes, our employees combined. We were discussing business until his crazy wife, Tracy showed up. She said she got an STD from me. Edwin was mad and threatened to kill me. I took a gun out my pocket and shot him. I didn't kill him, it was self-defense!"

"Did Edwin put his hands on you?"

"No," Josh mellows down.

"Did he fire a gun at you?"

"No."

"Explain, how was that self-defense then?"

"He said he was going to kill me for touching his wife."

I'm beginning to lose my patience, "And what?"

Josh raises his voice, "Nothing! I shot his ass and took care of the witnesses too!"

I hear footsteps outside the door. I unlock it. Mitch comes in the room with police officers. The police surround Josh and put him in handcuffs.

Mitch and I leave the building. I show Mitch the recorded confession on my phone. I say, "The only thing we didn't get is why a strand of

Isabella's hair was at the scene."

10

Mitch and I later meet Josh in the

interrogation room. Mitch and I pace back in forth

in the room. Josh sits at a table in handcuffs.

Mitch says, "We have all the information we

need from you expect one thing, Isabella Trail."

"What about her?" Josh asks.

I cross my arms and stand still, "How about

why was her DNA found at the scene of the crime?

She's been dead a while."

Josh shrugs his shoulders, "I haven't seen her since I was a teenager. Maybe it was someone else."

Mitch shows him the ring, "Do you recognize this? We also found this next to a nasty piece of your gum."

"Yeah, so. I gave her a ring and she left me for my friend."

"And you killed her many years later, why?" I ask.

Josh laughs hysterically, "I didn't kill her, she committed suicide!"

Mitch raises his voice, "Why was her DNA found at your crime scene!?"

Josh continues to laugh.

Mitch slams his fist on the table. Josh jumps.

Josh rolls his eyes, "You and I both know, the ring and gum are old. We had a connection back in the day. I have nothing to do with her death. Maybe one of my psycho ex-girlfriends or friends do and they're trying to distract you."

He has a point. I reply, "What friend or ex do you think?"

Josh shrugs his shoulders, "I don't know man. Tracy was psycho. My last girlfriend wouldn't."

"Veronica?"

"Yeah, yeah."

"Do you know where I can find either?"

"Tracy works at a salon on sixth street. Veronica cleans apartments for a living, she could be anywhere."

Mitch checks the time on his phone and looks at me. I take that as a cue to go. Mitch and I thank Josh and leave the building.

Mitch looks up something on his phone he says, "The salon isn't far from here." We walk to the salon.

A lady at the front desk asks if either one of us have an appointment. I shake my head. Mitch replies, "No, we're looking for Tracy."

The lady says, "That would be me. What do you want?"

I ask, "Do you know someone named Josh Richardson?"

Tracy is annoyed, "Yeah, I know him why? He gave me a disease and killed my husband! Who are you anyway?"

Mitch answers, "We're with the SIS, we're investigating the crime."

Tracy is quiet for a moment. She clears her voice, "Okay, I hope you don't think I did anything. The only thing I'm guilty of is coming near that creep."

"We don't. We're wondering if you have any information."

Tracy sighs, "Nope. Josh fired at my husband and I ran. I saw a blue haired lady run past me. I assumed it was another one of his girlfriends. Anything else?"

"Nope, that's all. Thank you," Mitch replies. We leave the salon and walk around the city.

I say, "Where do you think Veronica is?"

"Anywhere. You had a run in with her, you tell me?"

"I know she drinks and rides the bus."

"So, you want to go out tonight?"

"Sure."

Mitch and I head home. Later we meet up at the same pub I was at with Leanna last weekend.

Mitch and I sit at a table and wait. Cameron walks in the pub with Veronica. They sit behind us. I wink at Mitch. We hide our faces behind the menu and listen.

Cameron says, "So, tomorrow we're going to the beach?"

Veronica answers, "Sure."

"Have you seen those goons around lately?"

"No."

"Good. They got me fired. Terrible agents, really. They don't know the answer is in front of their face."

"What do you mean?"

"Nothing, I was drunk one night and saw Isabella walking the street. She resisted me."

It is quiet for a moment. The waiter comes over and takes their order. Veronica says, "I didn't think of you as a killer, you know."

A waiter comes over to our table. He asks, "Did you decide yet?"

I lower the menu away from my face and shake my head. Mitch puts his down. He gets up and goes over to Cameron and Veronica's table.

Mitch is firm, "Talk."

Cameron is amused, "Fine, you're terrible at your job!"

"You killed Isabella Trail."

"Maybe, maybe not. I was drunk! She said she didn't want to go home with me and ran away. I followed her, she still resisted me!"

"Then what? You killed her!?" Mitch raises his voice.

"Kill, is a strong word. I choked her, threw her in the water, and walked away. It's not my fault she couldn't swim!"

"That's not how the court is going to see it."

Mitch reaches in his pocket and plays back what Cameron said. Veronica storms out. I follow her.

Veronica notices. She turns around, "You're always following me. I have nothing to do with any of this. I wanted to see where Josh was going and I followed him. I didn't know he killed those people. I ran away when I saw the bodies."

I sigh, "Okay, I believe you but if we find out you're lying; there's going to be trouble."

"I don't know anything about Isabella Trail. All I know, the last two men I dated sucked. I wish I could help more but I can't," Veronica shrugs her shoulders.

The police arrive. Mitch meets me outside. I wave goodbye to Veronica. I tell Mitch what she said on the way to our cars.

Mitch says, "I don't believe Veronica would try to frame Isabella. We have zero evidence if she did. We have our people; we should be happy."

"Yeah," I smile.

Mitch notices, "We make a good team."

"I guess," I'm sarcastic.

"Maybe we should watch some lame crime movie where the agents investigating the crime end up together," Mitch winks.

I laugh, "Is that supposed to be a pick-up line?"

"Maybe."

"Sure."

Mitch leans over to kiss me.

One Year Later

Mitch and I never found out why Isabella's hair was at the warehouse. Makes me wonder if a spirit could leave clues in a crime scene. We will never know.

Duncan found out Rosa is his daughter. Since then, Duncan adopted her and she moved to Ireland with him. Mitch and Duncan are friends. We visit them a few times a year, or they'll visit us when Duncan has business in America.

Leanna and Nick are together. Josh and Cameron are locked up. Mitch and I are in charge of SIS. We're training some new agents to work on cases when we're out. I'm eight months pregnant for our first child, a daughter. Her name is going to be Bella Rose Levine Davis.